Dinosaur Countdown

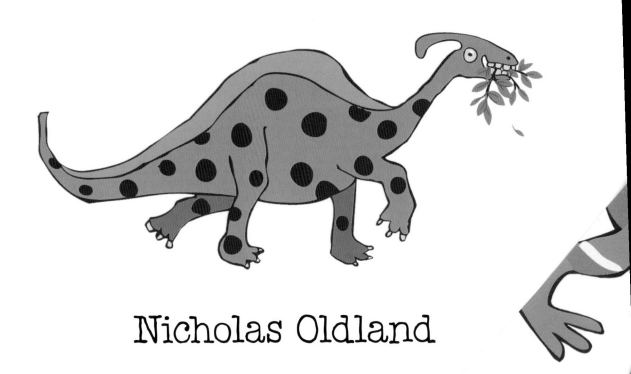

Nicholas Oldland

Kids Can Press

ten

striding velociraptors
(and one looming predator)

9

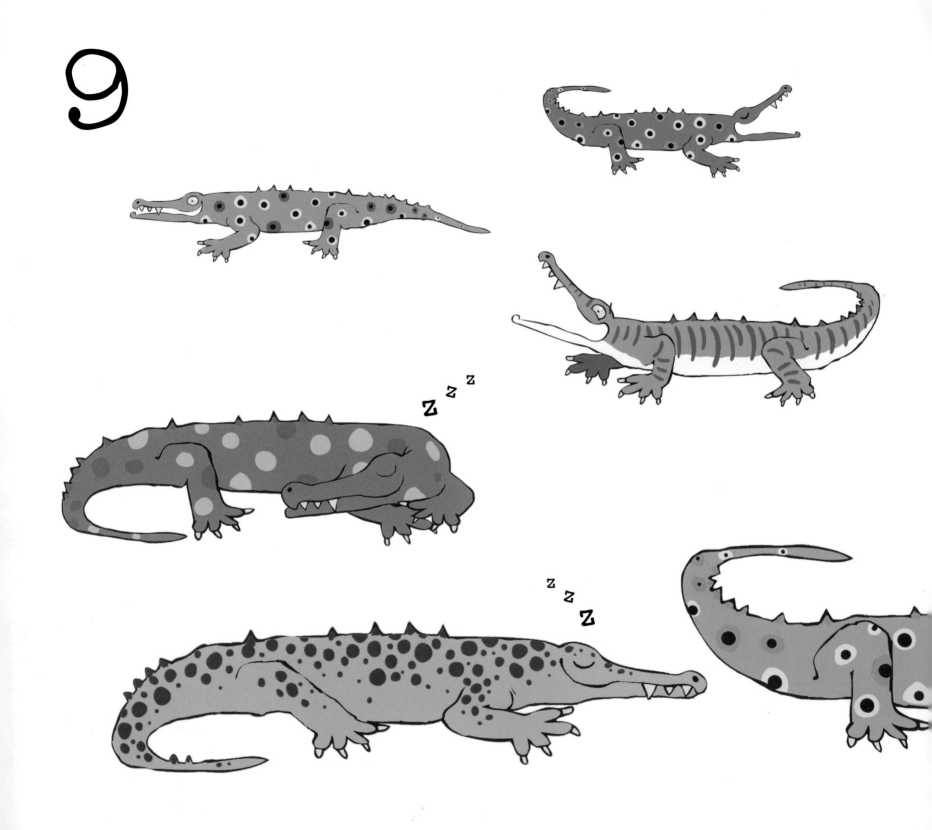

nine
lazing deinosuchus

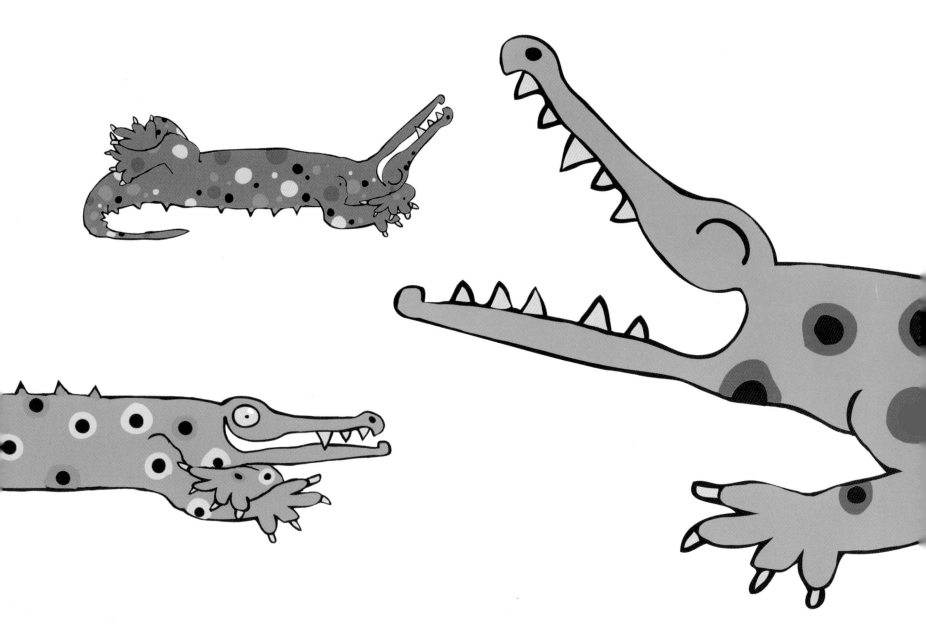

8

eight

munching herbivores

seven

sauntering parasaurolophus

(and what's that flying overhead?)

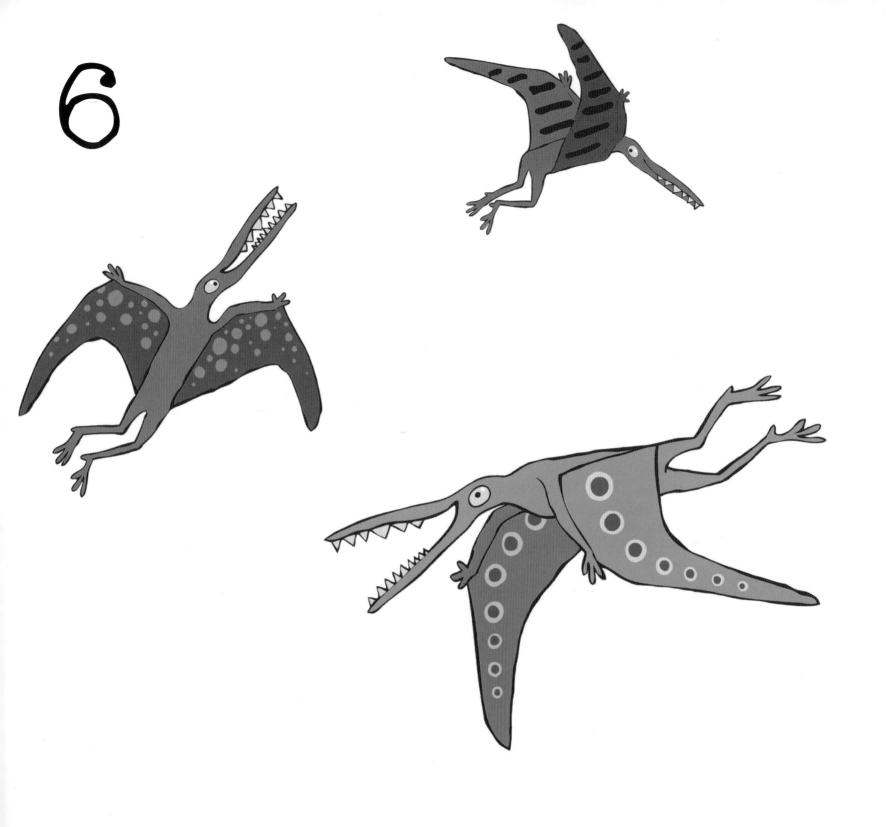

six

soaring pterodactyls

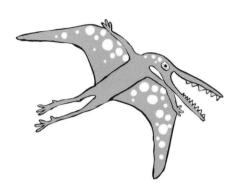

5

five

smiling deinonychus

four
roaring carnivores

3

three

rearing
dinosaurs

two

towering
tyrannosaurus

1

one
lumbering stegosaurus

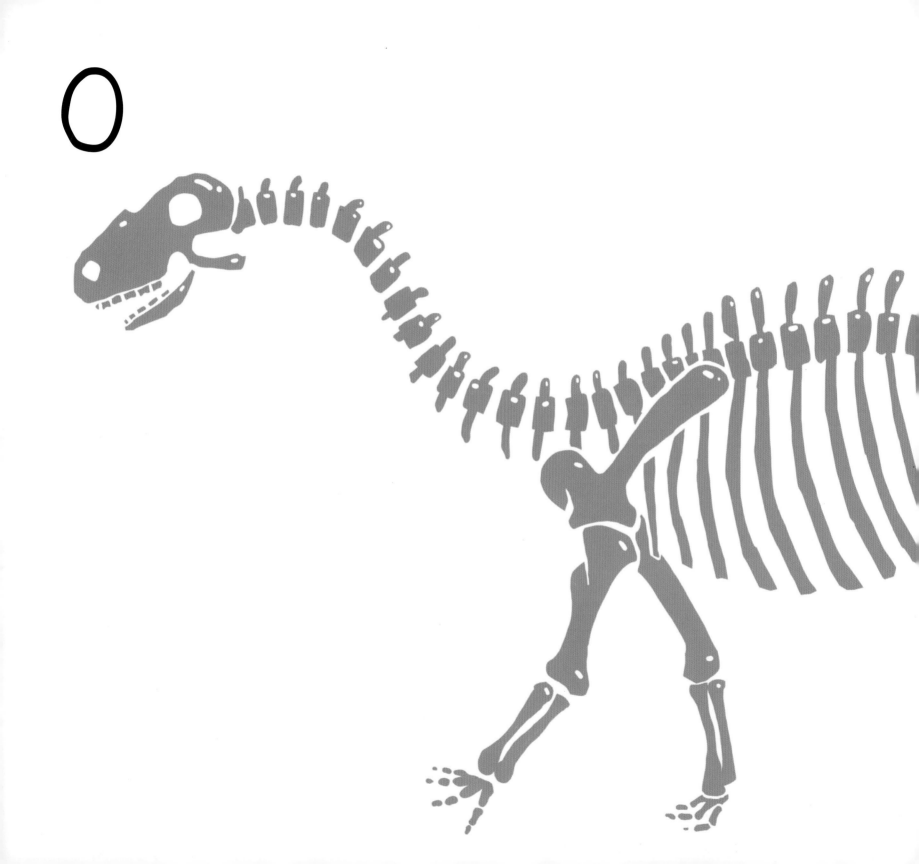

none

no dinosaurs
(they're extinct, silly!)

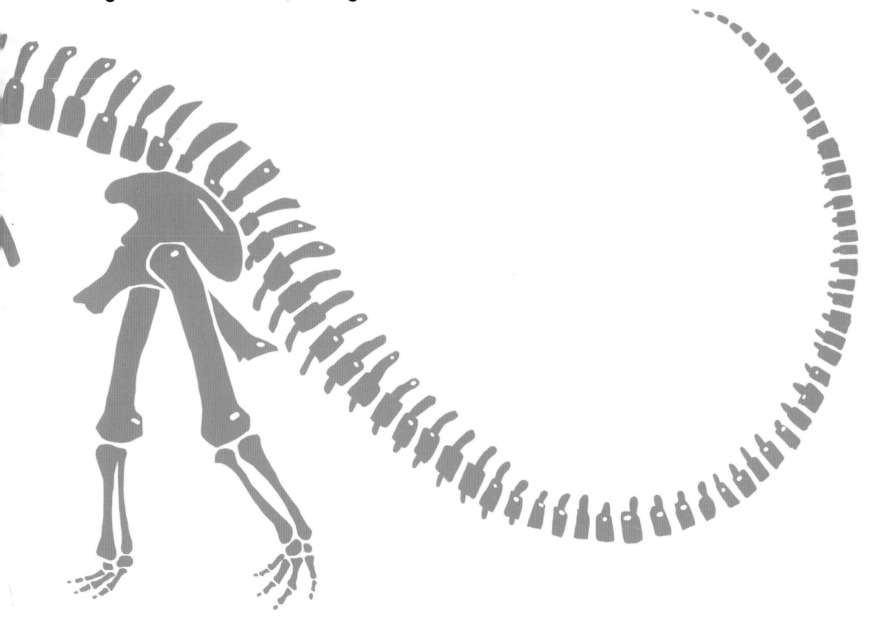

To Chloe, Eric and Sarah

Here's how you say the dinosaur names in this book:

Velociraptor	Veh-loss-ih-RAP-tore
Deinosuchus	Dye-NUH-suh-kus
Parasaurolophus	PAIR-ah-SORE-all-uh-FUS
Pterodactyl	Tair-uh-DAK-til
Deinonychus	Dye-NON-uh-kus
Tyrannosaurus	Tie-RAN-uh-SORE-us
Stegosaurus	Steg-uh-SORE-us

• •

Kids Can Press acknowledges the financial support of the Government of Ontario, through the Ontario Media Development Corporation's Ontario Book Initiative; the Ontario Arts Council; the Canada Council for the Arts; and the Government of Canada, through the BPIDP, for our publishing activity.

Published in Canada by
Kids Can Press Ltd.
25 Dockside Drive
Toronto, ON M5A 0B5

Published in the U.S. by
Kids Can Press Ltd.
2250 Military Road
Tonawanda, NY 14150

www.kidscanpress.com

The artwork in this book was rendered in Adobe Photoshop.
The text is set in Office Blogger.

Edited by Yvette Ghione
Designed by Julia Naimska

This book is smyth sewn casebound.
Manufactured in Singapore, in 3/2012
by Tien Wah Press (Pte) Ltd.

CM 12 0 9 8 7 6 5 4 3 2 1

FSC
www.fsc.org
MIX
Paper from
responsible sources
FSC® C019704

Library and Archives Canada Cataloguing in Publication

Oldland, Nicholas, 1972–
    Dinosaur countdown / Nicholas Oldland.

ISBN 978-1-55453-834-8

    1. Counting — Juvenile literature. 2. Dinosaurs — Juvenile literature. I. Title.

QA113.O55 2012   j513.2'11   C2011-908344-2

Kids Can Press is a *l©rus*™ Entertainment company